American built: dams

the debut collection of poetry by Siobhan Flynn.

contents

thanks   i

preface   iii

tears in a soon-to-be-basin   1

the night of Krrish

salt water

Schrodinger

chip

kingdom, i come

i want to read, perched on a cloud

stim

dipped

background dealer

desert

cold brew and coming back

a man known to American tradition

over yonder, child

she wouldn't go for that

660

i offend

go down

Panama

they pay $10 an hour at the colosseum

Hoover dam

Gatorade

cornered Earth

welcome, Joe Biden

America, as an island

thanks

to all the lands and the oceans in between

and all their dwellers that nudge their borders every day.

preface

I frequently bring up America in my poetry. I tend to stay away from America when exploring other modes of art, but for some reason, this often ends up being the place that I come to complain about the country I live in.

Living on this land, I often feel that I am surrounded by the other countries of the world all staring at me, shaking their heads. At the same time, I am told to be grateful by my mother and others that worked quite hard for the opportunity just to be allowed to be here.

For those that know me, my frequent groaning towards the end of political talks is expected. I often feel trapped in a mad house, different screams coming at me from every which way, no clear intentions from anyone, and little hope that anything good will emerge from it eventually. Nowadays, it almost seems like children in a bouncy house would be a more apt comparison.

In 2014 I watched a 9-minute short documentary directed by Emily Driscoll, *Invisible Ocean: Plankton and Plastic*. This, among other films and docs I saw that year at the annual Princeton Environmental Film Festival dug the pit in my stomach a little deeper.

Now, whenever I wash my clothes or my dishes or take my trash out, I wonder how many microplastics will travel to the ocean, suffocating and killing off the ocean's supply of phytoplankton – microscopic organisms that are responsible for producing 70% of the air we breathe, forget about the Amazon (you shouldn't actually though).

When I see cleaning efforts and smiling people collecting garbage along ocean shores, I wonder if they know how much damage has been done beyond their naked eye. I wonder if they know how much more plastic is still drifting past the horizon line.

What I have noticed after putting this collection together is that there are a few instances and interactions related to water that had a profound impact on my life. They gave perspectives that I've gone on to carry for over 10 years in some instances. I reflect on my time in Nepal and in Cape Cod; places I occasionally visited throughout my childhood. I also talk about life in my hometown over the years, specifically the devastating flooding it often faces. Moving from place to place, I've realized that the peoples' relationship with water can often people be drastically different.

There seems to be this sort of gap, even for the ones that seem to understand some of the greater forces at work around them. The thing is, even then they don't understand it. They just see it and want to slap a Band-Aid™ over it. They don't live it and dwell on any consequences. What gets in the way? Britas, water balloons, Hydroflasks, waterparks, SeaWorld. What do these things have in common? Brands, industry, capitalism, commercials, smiles. Something essential to life with a barcode attached to it.

The idea of a dam has always seemed very American to me. The size and magnitude of some of them and how effective they are at completely altering direction and focus. Dams bombard the entire world, significantly shifting all that was known before.

Americans run down lands the same way they construct their dams. Choosing the spots that work best for them, often causing the beauty and ways of life around them to wither and die. Dams displace and murder entire species of plants and animals and are just another iteration of Americans putting their noses where they don't belong, cutting off life support to those that lived there before them; those that appreciated the land before them.

They champion locations and hotspots like the Grand Canyon, all while continuing to defend the constructs that are slowly causing the landmark to decay. Thanks to dams, some communities have taken off and flourished while others that took millions of years to naturally turn into something meaningful and essential are quickly abolished. There is a lot of irony in dams.

This collection is not all that much about environmentalism, though it may not seem that way so far. If anything, I reflect on my unconscious abandonment of environmentalism as I have slowly understood that no matter what actions and no matter how many are taken, are all futile. No matter what is done, there is already a chance that my later years life will become expensive, uncomfortable, hot, and buried under blizzards.

Americans' inability to understand these concepts – in fact, their refusal to understand these concepts is just another shining example of their stubbornness that will slowly strangle everyone left on this planet.

Environment aside, I find it interesting how Americans see and understand their resources and everyday products that they have been unknowingly gifted with. The fact that they fail to realize the greater forces at work, many of them all being tied back to water – something essential in gallons and tons – is quite alarming.

The way they use and abuse many of the other things they can get their hands on is disgraceful from the perspective of most of the other inhabitants on this planet. I often find it difficult to think about this and express my feelings on this I often opt to avoid the contemplations all together. In a way, this is a release of my own dam – contemplations on my upbringing, my travels, and the country I love, but often want to escape.

tears in a soon-to-be-basin

the night of Krrish

in Nepal
i was in Nepal
haven't been there for so long

of the things that stand out

i would watch Power Rangers upstairs
with my cousins
my aunt screaming that
the food was ready.

when Krrish came out
everyone was over at the house.
there was a projector
bodies crowded
blank, empty faces
staring at a wall
in a darkened room
slack jawed for hours.

we were walking down Ring Road

i was tickled by the idea

of the three-wheeled tuk-tuk.

my amusement was gone

as my little eyes scanned

and i saw a man

crossing the street

with just his hands,

arms

his only limbs.

in this place,

surrounded by forest.

it looks like jungle

surrounded us for miles,

mist creeping up on us

shrouding us.

forcing us to huddle together,

creeping up slow enough to not pose any immediate threat.

hungry

in the jungle.

mother grabs a banana,

hands it to her daughter

she wants to feed me.

out of the mist springs a monkey!

"DAAIII!"

she cried in fear

snatching the banana

turning me away.

a mother's instinct

a survival instinct

almost her own undoing.

i was wandering back inside at night.

the night of Krrish.

we were saying goodbye to our friends and family

a sleepy girl, wandering inside from the gate, a few yards.

fumbling through the overgrown garden

– monsoon

it was wet.

elephant ears splashing

dripping,

showering an infant.

a huge heavy teardrop

landing on my arm

why

does it feel like that?

i didn't even scream

my mouth wide open,

no sound

no effort to be heard

horror by myself

in my own way.

a slug

thick slimy mystery.

no eyes,

no devious grin

no direction,

no motivation

a watery villain traveling up my arm

intentions unclear

salt water

the summer months call
for everyone on the east coast
to clamor to Jersey

Cape May
Wildwood
Point Pleasant
Bradley Beach
sometimes Seaside

chubby man child, reclining in your Tommy Bahama fold
away chair
red belly boiling and blistering in the summer sun
you pretend to sleep under Aviators while your wife
screams

there are children everywhere
they are sprinting through sands and dunes
pails flailing, waving their shovels
ready to dig into some hot summer fun

the children leap into the water

small feet pattering and slapping against the tacky wet sand,

little waves coming to greet them

for us it's normal,

after a while annoying.

sometimes i think it's like a nature program

like watching a herd of buffalo running across plains

some innate need to run under the Sun

an unspeakable yearning

driving them

keeping them in unison

pulling them to the salty seas.

one summer in Nepal, we climbed up this mountain

a quaint monastery was our summit for the day.

it was moist, misty

we stepped through an innocent, untouched creek.

after hiking down, we boarded a tuk-tuk.

my mother screamed.

these little black worms dangled from her ankles.

in her backpack

she produced tiny salt packets,

sprinkling the leeches

that had waited their entire lives in these small streams

waiting for something, someone

meaningful to latch onto

the leeches were tiny,

they could have been plucked off

just to be safe she sprinkled them, scorched them

shook them off,

kicked them away

get lost.

how are Americans toiling in the Jersey Shore sands

any different?

any more important?

than some leeches lying in wait for a little meal

no different than some little kiddos

waiting for the salty ocean to swallow them whole

waiting for Nature,

to play their part

kick them down,

sprinkle them with some salt

Schrodinger

i was awake for only a few moments before screaming
shrill cries and sobs
i pushed them out, belting
begging to be held, cradled

in the Oldsmobile
snuggled in a car seat
safe and sound
an uninterrupted ride,
hoping to guarantee a lifetime

i remember reaching,
grasping for the buckle,
a release.
it was centimeters away
the red clip
my fingers were itching,
begging to let me burst forth
ready to be born.

it seemed hours later

my father released me from this sweaty cell

"sorry, we didn't want to wake you yet,

we wanted to let you sleep a little longer"

the drive to the Cape was long, arduous

a journey, maybe 9 hours

with hand cranked windows.

towards the end

you're stiff and tired

and ready for the whole thing to be over with

but i was stuck too long

something was wrong

in a limbo

a car seat, a safe space

keeping me in its clutches,

saying my life is too precious

to let me go

already crying before my head popped out.

chip

bare feet on rocks

hard pebbles contorting your soles

you can't pretend like you enjoy it

a new summer,

a new evening

i trot around this sea glass beach with my mom and my
aunt

a forgiving crunch under my tiny toes

almost like dishes scraping against each other

or nails on a chalkboard

but it doesn't make you cringe

it helps you relax,

breathe out

and breath in the air on a Cape Cod beach

the air gives you this dizzying feeling

as you glance across a spectacle of oblong colors

real life impressionism.

people love to grab the colorful ones

mostly blue and green

but sometimes pink and orange.

when the vacationers have gone

i'd imagine there are cream-colored piles

idling at the shore

waiting to get washed,

rung out again

bring me back

something better next year.

kingdom, i come

when i got to the beach
i wanted to go home
far away from Ocean Grove
into the depths with bubbling corals
and laughing horses

if i swam out far enough
if i held my breath underwater,
did 10 somersaults in a row
without getting dizzy
– the secret recipe to sprouting gills

my mermaid mentor
come fetch me at the shore
i'm ready, waiting to swim away
thousands of miles and miles
to my real home, layered in blues

i want to read, perched on a cloud

days and weekends when i can't
find a good spot to read
when i can't tend to my work

i think about picking up a book for some time
relaxing and getting comfortable.
there's something about my desk
and the library makes me agitated
those bright fluorescent lights
the sniffling and sighing
the heaviness of everyone's workload combined
in old buildings
no ventilation
no new ideas
can't shake the nerves eating at me

i pull on a thin pair of gloves and sunglasses
wrap my neck in a scarf and sit in one of the Adirondacks
with my laptop

this isn't great,

but it's better.

just as i start to feel cold and my fingers feel stiff,

the winds biting me in the ass has me on a roll,

sprinting to a finish line

a deadline.

after i finish this piece i'll pack up and go sit on the
radiator.

i want to read some poetry now

i'm out of ideas.

i forced out these words and similes from

shaking, hypothermic hands

moving

and typing

because stillness means

you're dead in the water

i want to float away

up and up

perch on a cloud

sit under the Sun

turning pages for days

thawing my fingers

warming my heart

cure some of that desperation.

i want to rain down in the evening

when i'm heavy with emotion.

i want to bathe the world in my words.

stim

i'm drowning in some quiet awareness.
life is going on
leaving without me
that last ferry out
a trail of maddening bubbles
not fizzling out soon enough
still the only sound echoing for miles
and the only reminder

an hourglass sprinkled across the water
i'll be alone soon

dipped

i was sick last week
i missed our first week on the water.

waiting at the boat house
peeling my sneakers off at the docks
shedding a sweater
getting ready to plow through the cold airs
sneaking up on the Charles
in the middle of October

1
starboard
the coxswain had a microphone
but i still felt like i heard her a millisecond too late

i couldn't move in time
scared to dip my oar in the water
the weakling of the batch,
strategically and purposely placed
at the back of the pack.
falling behind,

will that one make it?

she'll need some sort of miracle to help her catch up to all
her brothers and sisters

if she has any hope of making it through the winter.

the first time i lost my timing

my oar punched me in the gut

knocked out my confidence

the second time it didn't hurt as bad

but my coach glared at me across the water

a disapproving glare,

a disappointed mother duck

not sure whether she should keep wasting her time

knowing in soon she'd have to tend to her more promising
younglings

the third time

i was thrown

flung into frigid waters

looked at

laughed at.

i didn't even struggle

i waded for a moment

i knew i had lost

i fell too far behind

and now i was ready to sink to the bottom of the Charles

failed one of the litter.

background dealer

………..

i can't sit with my own mind

can't enjoy the peace of this infinitely stilling river.

can't hop on this train

ride to enlightenment,

Eden

i look everywhere

anywhere

thinking up sounds

voices

villains in my mind,

perfect to keep me running down the banks.

maybe jump in

take a chance

bet

lottery

why not?

i haven't got a job,

i need a job

i can't set my mind to anything,

i'm overcrowding this conscious

looking for excuses, just a number of imaginations

their existence alone

giving me a social pass

conversational gas

why am i plagued

with the task of purpose

i've been trying so hard

without one break

in a stream of consciousness,

building a raging river in my mind

the perfect excuse to fall overboard

and never come up.

if i do

i'll be the hero

i'll be a bird on a buoy

a symbol of a resilience,

the dove.

i'll have a job,

a purpose.

it's my turn

to drown you out.

desert

my feet were burning, boiling

walking with the weight of my children.

my children,

my life's work

my pride and joy

nowhere to be seen.

this ornate figure is

a foreshadowing,

some abstract expanse

that's pleasing to the eye,

somewhere retaining endless lives

45 - 11

= 34

34 × 12

= 408

408 ÷ 10

(to be gracious,

a month for recovery)

that leaves

at least

40

blistering

cracking

cackling

this aging weight,

i'm getting lighter every month.

the weight of the world

my life's worth

getting smaller

shorter.

it's my time to start

my 1/40

22 years left

23 years spent

1/40

- 1/40

= 0

i'm going backwards

leaning and stumbling

fumbling for someone

to have my back

give me a chance

to do something

right by myself.

another 1/40,

still not worth it.

cold brew and coming back

forcing water to maneuver through
coffee grounds
faster, faster
man-made fire
man made fire
man made instant coffee.

something about
letting water go on its own
doing as it pleases
its own free will

the best, the strongest,
the surest coffee
presented by Nature.
the finest version
the purest nectar
takes time and patience
beyond the lifespan of
a too slow human

trapped in a forlorn
kingdom

a man known to American tradition

what constitutes meeting someone?

what are the criteria for your awareness for you to
accurately state

"yes, i knew that man"?

my grandfather died when i was 2

i guess i met him

there are pictures of us together

posed like world leaders

getting together in a shot

holding hands

at least one gazes into the camera

"yes, i know him now"

we are friends, for you.

i met him, but i never knew him.

there was a cottage in Cape Cod

Jerry, he built these dressers, painted on beautiful tulips

intertwined pink buds elegantly

sprawling up a vanity

matching the sheets, too

after he was gone, we took turns

"yeah, we're staying at the Cape"

i never met him,

but the calm i felt when i ran my fingers

across these hand painted yellowy white dressers.

the time bounding through me,

poured out from his soul

the skill

the labor

the dedication.

an American family

bound for the ocean

looking out at this body of water,

jumping forth into the body of water

that carried us here.

i never met him,

but he reminded me of these men from textbooks

Founding Fathers.

a hand carved wooden sign hanging outside the cottage
door.

"FLYNN"

our declaration of summer getaway independence.

i never met him,

but he created a world for me.

i can't thank him,

i don't even know if i like it sometimes,

but he is another great

another poised gentleman

in a sepia portrait

smiling on

grin cast across the Atlantic.

over yonder, child

another summer out on the Cape
another day, another burn
another set of red cheeks,
another disgruntled sigh from mom

i was a sea captain that day,
red cheeks were excusable.
how can i hold the grit of a seaman
while my mother fusses over my 70 SPF?

when you're a child, you tune out what they say about the
other kids
that's why i have no recollection of a voice over the
intercom saying
"get in line behind the captain
if you want to give your kid a chance to steer."

my body was slumping downward between my armpits
i was getting too old to be carried like this
but to me, i stood alone
tall

proud

no other kids in line

not even a kid myself.

if i was a child why did i feel a sad longing

when i scanned the bay

sea breeze scattering some curls

i squinted, diligent at my post

and saw two whales flipping over across the water

in real time, they moved in slow motion

they took too long,

long enough for me to ponder whether they were

flying or flailing

long enough for a little girl to realize

this helm wasn't real

she wouldn't go for that

i don't drink soda.
i hate the taste,
the feeling too
it's like drinking chaotic mud water
sludge.

people love it so much,
they'll pump it with aspartame
just to excuse their hold on this beverage
a brown boiling filth

just find a way to put it on a paper
a logo
red, white, and blue
something inspiring
something immortal
something evolved
something American,
lethal.

built on grit.

poor

dirt

scum.

you love to hate

you'd be bored without it.

i only drink water,

even here that's rare.

safety of water

safe water

pure water.

water,

tainted with oil

sludge

bubbles

sea birds picking at your leftovers.

spillage

poison.

lethal.

660

i've waited tables

served many hungry people

many juicy burgers

in different restaurants

in different cities

some things never change

every time i bus my tables

i bring back the dishes

scrape more plates

napkins, toothpicks,

gum wrappers

fall into the garbage.

then down plop handfuls of pasta

tomatoes from a salad

a squeezed lemon, with barely a dent

10 bites of a burger

and half of the table's vegetable portions

on a trip to the dish station

i've learned to empty my gaze.

once or twice in the past

peering into the garbage too long

caused a few tears to well up

those tears are nothing compared

to the gallons and gallons,

metric tonnes of water

washed away

dirtied and poisoned

brethren meeting their maker in a landfill.

it takes 660 gallons of water to put a burger on your plate.

it's like Mary Poppins

this bottomless garbage can at the back of the restaurant.

good thing you can't pull out a mirror

to see your whole face

would you be able to look at yourself

if you saw the oceans you've poured into black plastic
bags?

i offend

i offend
i say to friends,
would you like to hear a story?

i tell them of other lands,
other receptacles,
other ways.
they recoil,
offended
by the mere thought of something done differently
especially when it's done better.

they hated stories about composting
until they're 20 and they want a fun word to add to their
skills, qualities.

hey everyone,
i'm a composter now.
a poster child for
"i thought of it myself!
all on my own!"

everyday,

a comment about how my water bottle is always at my side

a comment about the nice color i picked out.

you never see anything for what it is,

just how you can layer it with other feathers

your identity

your coat, cover

a promise,

there's something good under here

go down

the drop off

the end

the edge of a dam

the space where you tell your kids not to go

who knows where the waters will drag them from there

heaven, hell

unfortunate headline

a lost child, or a lost planet

but hold on to your industry

Panama

when i first learned
about Panama Canal
i was excited by the profound change
to how we traveled an expanse
that makes up 70% of the surface surrounding us

just draw the edge of an eraser
millimeters over a map

less time
less resources too

but as i've gotten older
as i've understood 20 something years around me
and years further back behind my existence
manifesting greed time after time
always hungrier than the years prior

getting little stickers on your homework once a week
you want more stickers
get more stickers

one day maybe it'll be something special, different.

so you get a big ice cream sundae after school
another day at work and then everything changes.

big will never be your biggest
each time you win
you only see losses
until your next sundae.

they pay $10 an hour at the colosseum

today at work in the middle of July

my friend and i dragged a bucket

into a supply closet

twisting and gritting our teeth

have you ever tried using one of those water balloon
nozzles?

kids on their bathroom breaks

coming up behind me

poking me in the shoulder

when will they be ready?

can i hold one?

can i touch it?

we lug this bucket

full of water balloons

little sacs of malice

full of waste

full of violence

full of spite,

a catharsis for the kiddos

that want to whip their least favorite playmate in the face

we offer them a huge bucket

a party-size cooler

go, reach in a grab

giggle as their arm comes back

ready to hurl some hate

grinning as they make a major league impact

probably somewhere in the grass

their hands are tainted

not bloodstained, yet

lying in the grass

a disfigured fluorescent worm

a piece of wreckage

a souvenir that will take thousands of years to decay.

a readiness to knock down and destroy

with anything

by any means

Hoover dam

industry, innovation, invigoration
strong walls
strong values

will we ever have enough walls?

dams, river walls
ocean walls, levees
people walls, borders

creating jobs
employing people you impoverished
on their own lands
filling their pockets
for some time.
drying out their river.

your name on a dam,
mother, i made it!
i would be offended
scared,

ashamed at the idea.

an immortal name on a concept

that dwarts the common person,

dividing life and death

choosing death for life.

Gatorade

recently

i learned a placebo is not a placebo.

when used as a placebo

the notion of it affects the effect

my cousin handed me

yellow Gatorade.

i was curled up on the floor

it was raining outside

i was looking up at the TV.

here we had HBO East, HBO West

if you miss it

you can come back in three hours,

try to catch it the second time around.

for some reason i remember watching *Chucky*,

giving up on Go-Fish

"this will help you, this will fix it"

it was monsoon

something about that made the stomach bug worse

something about the water

something in the water

Westerners can't handle.

the disease of my dad.

"drink it, drink the Gatorade"

this fluorescent elixir

will swirl through my stomach

will travel far and wide across a mesentery

smiting

biting

eradicating.

beating up devil's spawn

like the green goblin from Mucinex ads,

paid for by Reckitt Benckiser.

a cute little creeper

made for pharma propaganda.

knock it out

a bug, an illness

bread in the water.

when you leave your home,

your clipped lawns

and suburbs

the kind of place where your water qualms get national coverage,

visits from Mr. Obama

when you leave your home,

waters wash over you

a reaper dispatched by Mother nature.

either your smiling TV sports drink will save you

from drowning

in more of these angry waters.

Atlantic to Pacific

these waters are boiling for the white man.

cornered Earth

in that corner of the universe…

in this corner of the universe

our jargon contradicts

the science.

a result of blood, sweat, tears

generations of advancement

in this corner of the universe, we hold flat Earther
conventions

a testament to the plateau,

flatlining of human advancement

conspiracies lighting up minds

lighting up cell towers

out of fear of lizards

you know,

the kinds that put 5G chips in your phones

to activate the virus.

Kingsman,

yeah, i saw that one in theaters

in this corner of the universe

we improve technology to express our fear of it

millions of dollars to program

a deadly, lifelike AI

soon she won't just be on screen.

the more you manifest your imaginations,

feared ideations

in this corner of the universe

we blasted off and away

not making it to another corner yet,

so who could've assigned these dimensions anyways?

dimensional universe

and a humdrum mind

cornering themselves

destroying spaceships

that have been under construction since the dawn of time

welcome, Joe Biden

Trumpist

leftist

screaming, crying

drowning, dying

the likes of both

waves crashing down on your homes,

seeping through basement cracks

silently

swiftly

striking you down.

bringing out the worst in both.

Manville, NJ.

a miserable victim

unable to move forward,

never going backward enough.

is it the phonies, the politics?

the red surrounded by blue?

or is it just the Blue

crashing down on you

taking you and your loved ones

pulling you into a raging river

locking you in your room, no dinner

letting your roof, your house crash down around you

your Freedom fortress reduced to rubble.

welcome, Joe Biden

help us, Joe Biden

this is America

your America.

here we are not red, white, and blue

these days we ask

are we red

or are we blue?

but most of us are just white…

welcome, Joe Biden

tell us, Joe Biden

about these funds

promised long before Floyd.

i saw you appear,

but did you show up?

please, Joe Biden

build us an arc,

or drown us in promises

photo-ops

make-nice handshakes

.

America, as an island

there is a jealousy of the oceans
running down deeper than Marianas Trench

in America there are walls being put up everywhere
there are political campaigns run on the concept of a wall
a testament to all, we are capable of
creating something that can tower over us
– giving birth to giants

giant hurricanes
a three-hundred-mile-wide army
storming the shores,
storming on our States.
no matter how many times a city is submerged
it will rise again
higher than before,
to be arranged with your contractor.

greenhouse gasses,
they say this is the cause of the oceans rising
whether or not you choose to know science,

the oceans

are

rising.

we are one of the few powerful nations

refusing to believe that.

the byproducts of our favorite products

are isolating us

squeezing us inland

cutting us off from a world that has wanted

nothing to do with us for some time now.

i was born on this island

to a disgruntled American,

his mind placing him on an island of his own

back when we were less fearful of water

and more about the red vessels that lurked under it.

a distraction on our radar.

and to an immigrant,

now trapped here with a rising fear

of the people loudly embracing their rights and institutions

– the same ones that brought her here.

if i run away

will i be doing wrong by

the ones that are being pushed out,

drowning?

if i swim away

is there a reason why i should be trusted?

when i wash up

gasping, sputtering

desperately seeking

to be heard

in a world that believes

i'm from a land

that's missed the mark

that one day soon

may not even be marked on a map

forgotten, overtaken

and submerged

the land of the Free people.

humans when given free will

have an odd way of using it.

Made in the USA
Monee, IL
30 November 2021

4adf722a-c753-416f-88d9-7875831636ecR02